4|14

EssexWorks.
For a better quality of life

Please return this book on or before the date shown above. To
renew go to www.essex.gov.uk/libraries, ring 0845 603 7628 or
go to any Essex library.

Puff Flies

Level 3C

Written by Sally Grindley
Illustrated by Valentina Mendicino

Tick
Tock

What is synthetic phonics?

Synthetic phonics teaches children to recognise the sounds of letters and to blend 'synthesise' them together to make whole words.

Understanding sound/letter relationships gives children the confidence and ability to read unfamiliar words, without having to rely on memory or guesswork; this helps them progress towards independent reading.

Did you know? Spoken English uses more than 40 speech sounds. Each sound is called a *phoneme*. Some phonemes relate to a single letter (d-o-g) and others to combinations of letters (sh-ar-p). When a phoneme is written down it is called a *grapheme*. Teaching these sounds, matching them to their written form and sounding out words for reading is the basis of synthetic phonics.

Consultant

I love reading phonics has been created in consultation with language expert Abigail Steel. She has a background in teaching and teacher training and is a respected expert in the field of Synthetic Phonics. Abigail Steel is a regular contributor to educational publications. Her international education consultancy supports parents and teachers in the promotion of literacy skills.

Reading tips

This book focuses on the ie sound as in pies.

Tricky words in this book

Any words in bold may have unusual spellings or are new and have not yet been introduced.

Tricky words in this book:

**the   me   I   makes   into
look   to   was   your   he**

Extra ways to have fun with this book

After the reader has finished the story, ask them questions about what they have just read:

Why is Puff upset?
Who does Puff meet when he is flying?

Explain that the two letters 'ie' make one sound. Think of other words that use the 'ie' sound, such as *pie* and *cries*.

I am Puff's dad. Every night I listen to Puff read. He likes to sit on my lap when he reads.

A pronunciation guide

This grid highlights the sounds used in the story and offers a guide on how to say them.

s as in sat	a as in ant	t as in tin	p as in pig	i as in ink
n as in net	c as in cat	e as in egg	h as in hen	r as in rat
m as in mug	d as in dog	g as in get	o as in ox	u as in up
l as in log	f as in fan	b as in bag	j as in jug	v as in van
w as in wet	z as in zip	y as in yet	k as in kit	qu as in quick
x as in box	ff as in off	ll as in ball	ss as in kiss	zz as in buzz
ck as in duck	pp as in puppy	nn as in bunny	rr as in arrow	gg as in egg
dd as in daddy	bb as in chubby	tt as in attic	sh as in shop	ch as in chip
th as in them	th as in the	ng as in sing	nk as in sunk	le as in bottle
ai as in rain	ee as in feet	ie as in pies		

Be careful not to add an 'uh' sound to 's', 't', 'p', 'c', 'h', 'r', 'm', 'd', 'g', 'l', 'f' and 'b'. For example, say 'fff' not 'fuh' and 'sss' not 'suh'.

Puff **the** dragon lies on the grass and cries.

"Mum flies, Dad flies, but not **me**."

Puff sees Cat.

"Cat flies but not me!" Puff cries.

"**I** will help," Meg replies.

Meg **makes** a pie from dried frogs and fried snails.

"Fee, fie!" cries Meg.
Meg casts a spell on the pie.

Puff chomps on the pie.
Puff flies up **into** the skies!

"Mum! Dad!" Puff cries.
"This dragon flies!"

"The spell will not last long,"
Meg replies.

Puff spies a goblin.

"**Look** at me!" Puff cries.

Puff spies an elf.

"Look at me!" Puff cries.

The spell dies. Puff drops from the skies on **to** the grass.

"I wish I **was** still in the skies,"
Puff cries. "Just flap **your** wings,"
his mum replies.

Puff tries. **He** flaps his wings.

And off Puff flies!
Yippee!

OVER **48** TITLES IN SIX LEVELS
Abigail Steel recommends...

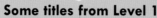

Some titles from Level 1

 Bad Rat

 The Best Gift

 Clint and Grant Play I-Spy

 Gran and Bret's Trip

978-1-84898-277-2   978-1-84898-396-0   978-1-84898-548-3   978-1-84898-547-6

Some titles from Level 2

 Wish Fish

 Chuck and Duck

 Pink Bunny

 Let's go to the Swings

978-1-84898-386-1   978-1-84898-387-8   978-1-84898-550-6   978-1-84898-549-0

Other titles to enjoy from Level 3

 Bart's Go-Cart

 Queen Ella's Feet

 Goat in a Boat

978-1-84898-552-0   978-1-84898-398-4   978-1-84898-400-4

An Hachette UK Company
www.hachette.co.uk

Copyright © Octopus Publishing Group Ltd 2012
First published in Great Britain in 2012 by TickTock, an imprint of Octopus Publishing Group Ltd,
Endeavour House, 189 Shaftesbury Avenue, London WC2H 8JY.
www.octopusbooks.co.uk

ISBN 978 1 84898 399 1

Printed and bound in China
10 9 8 7 6 5 4 3 2 1